Today Okay

by

Jacob M. Cheha

illustrated by Mark Pagano

Today's Okay

by

Jacob M. Cheha

illustrated by Mark Pagano

Today's Okay
To stand on my head
And sing to my Mom
'til my face is bright red

Today's Okay

To say how are you

In French, Farsi, Fijian

Mongolian and Hindu!

Today's Okay

To dress with a flair

In stripes and bright colors

And bows in your hair

Today's Okay
To walk in the rain
Splash in each puddle
and block every drain

Today's Okay

To listen in class

The students who don't

Will surely not pass!

Today's Okay

To ask lots of questions

The teacher is there

To give you suggestions

Today's Okay

To eat healthy food

You'll feel strong and mighty

And in a great mood

Today's Okay

To imagine the zoo

and jump 'round the park

like a big kangaroo

Today's Okay

To make some new buddies

Fun can be just as

Important as studies

Today's Okay

To get homework done

You might even find

That learning is fun!

Today's Okay
For playing outside
Go ahead swing on your swings
Or slide down your slide

Today's Okay

To say if you're mad

Take a breath, count to ten

It isn't so bad

Today's Okay

To go down for a snack

Mom and Dad will protect you

From a monster attack

Today's Okay
To snuggle and say
Sweet dreams bring you softly
To a new Okay Day!

9872238R0